The Grunt Factor

A wartime story of
excitement, danger, intrigue

by

Crisp E Bacon

Maurice Bird
Illustrated by Brenda Howden

Matador
5 Weir Road
Kibworth Beauchamp
Leicester LE8 0LQ, UK
Tel: 0116 279 2299
Fax: 0116 279 2277
Email: books@troubador.co.uk
Web: www.troubador.co.uk/matador

ISBN 978 1848763 531

British Library Cataloguing in Publication Data.
A catalogue record for this book is available from the British Library.

Typeset in 11pt Times by Troubador Publishing Ltd, Leicester, UK

Matador is an imprint of Troubador Publishing Ltd

Printed in Great Britain by the MPG Books Group, Bodmin and King's Lynn

To Nicole and Sam who gave me the inspiration

INTRODUCTION

Sir Winston Churchill who, in my opinion, namely the author, and most other characters in this book, was the finest person that ever lived.

More importantly he liked pigs. It was Sir Winston who said "Dogs look up to you, cats look down on you, but pigs treat you as their equal!"

Now please read on....

CHAPTER 1

It is War!

After a rather long and uneventful journey, the large, khaki camouflage clad car turned into the entrance of a very active wartime fighter station. It was a very famous station and the large sign outside the main gate confirmed this. "Welcome to RAF Piggin Hill."

No sooner had the car rolled to a halt when out clambered the chauffeur. However, before he had a chance to walk the few yards to the guard room, he was confronted by a very large guard brandishing a very highly polished stick towards his direction.

'Can I help you?' the guard asked somewhat gruntingly.

'As a matter of fact you can,' the chauffeur responded in what could be described as an authoritative tone.

He continued, 'In the rear of this vehicle sits someone who doesn't like to be kept waiting, you have probably heard of him, namely Air Commodore Sir Norman Thyne-Rashers, DFM, DSO and most other letters of the alphabet.'

Pigs by nature are not normally prone to panicking, and are rarely seen to be flustered, but here we have an exception.

'Er, h'mm, er, right away sir – guards – guards! Open the gate, jump to it, sorry sir, sorry, have you through in no time.'

The first guard, had by this time, gone a bright pink and was saluting everything in sight. Even the chauffeur, a mere leading aircraftsman, was receiving a fair share of the salutes being banded around. As for the VIP in the back of the car, he swore he could feel a draught from the guard's very aggressive trotter saluting action, even though the window was only slightly open.

The chauffeur, LAC Stacy, loved his job and always had a laugh when visiting places with his prominent rear seat passenger and watching the type of panic that always occurred in instances such as this. By the look of Sir Norman's expression through the rear mirror, the LAC didn't think he was on his own on that one.

War had been raging for a few years now so it wasn't surprising that security was tight, especially at establishments like RAF Piggin Hill. To gain access, two sets of gates had to be opened to allow traffic in and out, which involved four personnel to carry out the entering and leaving procedure.

With the original guard plus four others in attendance, things were buzzing. With chains rattling, keys clanking and sets of studded boots shuffling on hard tarmac, a normally peaceful part of the station had suddenly changed into one of noise and mayhem.

'Get those gates open,' the guard in charge yelled at the top of his voice. 'If you don't you will all be for the chop!'

Suddenly everyone stopped.

'Oops, sorry lads, shouldn't have mentioned the word chop, slip of the tongue, my apologies.'

You don't mention words like chop in Pigland, it's just not politically correct or PC as everyone now knows it by.

Fortunately the apology was accepted and, eventually, the car, and its contents, negotiated the elaborate system and were on their way to the destination – the Control Sty.

With no more gates or obstructions to pass through, the car drew up at what only can be described as an earth mound. As expected, though, it wasn't an ordinary mound because the moment the car pulled up, a large hole appeared on one side and a welcoming committee emerged from inside.

LAC Stacy was very au fait with such occurrences and in a flash had leapt from the car and was opening the rear door for his important passenger.

'Sir Norman, how the devil are you? Welcome to Piggin Hill, how was your trip?'

The words uttered came from the head of the welcoming committee, who was obviously a senior member of the Royal Pig Air Force, recognisable not only by a medal clad uniform but by the way he spoke and his appearance, top brass in other words.

'Jeremy,' the Air Commodore responded. 'Nice to see you old pig, how's that lovely wife of yours and those ten little squeakers?'

'Fifteen now Sir Norman, she had a litter last week, back at work now though.'

'You asked me about the trip Jeremy,' Sir Norman said remembering such a question had been asked. 'Well the answer is fine and uneventful until we got to your blessed main gates.'

Everyone present laughed, knowing what the Air Commodore and his chauffeur had experienced.

'Just wait until you try to get out,' someone retorted, which had everyone rolling about with laughter.

It is good to be able to share a spot of jovial banter in these troubled times and it makes no difference if you are humans or pigs.

The Control Sty had been hurriedly constructed at the beginning of the war, with everyone doing their bit. Twenty volunteers, no less, spent three weeks hewing the ground with their snouts and trotters. It wasn't just a matter of digging a

4

small hole, it had to be deep, very deep. It had to be undetectable and protected from any prying eye that might just fly over. No chances could be taken.

Of course, if you have a deep hole then you have to have ways and means to get up and down. This is where some of the best engineers in the Royal Pig Air Force Regiment came in. All qualified in their specific fields.

One of the engineers had spent a lot of his youth roaming about farmyards. The reason being he kept escaping from his sty due to a piece of rotted chicken wire pushed at the back to try and keep him and the other pigs in.

Being a small pig, he could wriggle through a small hole which appeared and basically had the freedom of Swine Farm. He was a canny sort of a pig and remained undetected for months, returning at will to enjoy the food delivered to the trough each day.

It was during his freedom he studied all aspects of farming and one thing he observed with interest had now come in useful at the airfield and in particular the Control Sty.

From the safety of a heap of straw bales, the young pig watched as sacks of corn were loaded on to a device and lifted into the air by winding a large handle. At the time the word on the side, "Sack Barrow" meant nothing at all but here it was to prove a very useful piece of equipment.

'Right, Sir Norman,' Jeremy said gesturing his guest, 'if you would like to climb aboard we'll go down to where all planning is carried out.'

As instructed, the Air Commodore stepped on to the modified barrow and his friend Jeremy joined him. He was then joined by other members of the welcoming party, leaving the chauffeur to find a suitable place for a well earned break. The NAAFI was the ideal place.

'Hold tight Gentlepigs,' the operator, a rather attractive female called. 'We're going down!'

With that, the young lady commenced winding a large handle which operated a ratchet carrying everybody to the depths of the Control Sty.

As is the case with any war organisation, control, good intelligence and strategy are paramount. Keeping yourself one step ahead of your enemy by finding out what they were planning always proved vital in any conflict. From the bowels of the earth in this remote airfield the outcome of the war could, and most certainly would, be decided.

Sir Norman Thyne-Rashers was keen to see how things were progressing for himself, hence the reason for his visit. From the large maps on the wall and the various coloured pins stuck in them, he could see how things were at that precise moment.

The coloured pins represented a number of things and his eyes were fixed in particular on the red ones. These indicated the movement of the enemy, whether it was aircraft, ships or

7

troops on the ground. Things didn't look very encouraging, in fact the situation was diabolical.

Jeremy Ridgeback, Wing Commander of some repute, who had greeted his old colleague on arrival to the Control Sty, beckoned Sir Norman over to a chart that was situated near one of the large maps.

'I think you ought to see this sir,' the Wing Commander said pointing with an indicator stick he had taken from a nearby table. 'Unfortunately due to the human situation, and by that I mean the lack of resources, they can no longer handle the intelligence side of things. As a result it has been handed over to us.'

'And how are we doing?' the Air Commodore enquired.

There was total silence except for the sound of deep sighs.

'Well?'

'I'm afraid it's not sir,' the Wing Commander had to admit in a dejected tone. He went on to explain further, 'Around six months ago the Ministry of Defence advised us we should form a new unit to take over "behind enemy line operations". This, as you know, is when we parachute some of our highly intelligent forces behind the enemy's lines to gather important data. Things like troop movement and hopefully things they are planning so we can hit them before they have a chance of putting it into operation.'

The Wing Commander stopped to take a breath before continuing in a subdued tone, 'I am afraid to say it sir, but since we pigs took over, not only has information dried up but we have lost all contact with everyone over there.'

'You mean they've all been killed or captured?'

'We have no idea sir,' Jeremy answered his friend. 'No one has heard from them for weeks.'

The situation was dire. Apart from being embarrassed at the total loss of information, unlike the great amount when the humans did the job, no one knew what had happened or, more to the point, what was happening. The outcome of the war could hinge on this whole dilemma.

The unit referred to was aptly named the S.H.S, or, to give it its full title, the Special Hog Service. It was, as mentioned earlier, made up of highly intelligent pigs who should be able to avoid detection behind enemy lines and yet get close enough to gather valuable information.

To illustrate this, one human early last year infiltrated a secret enemy strategic unit and fed back such valuable information. He was alone responsible for saving thousands of lives.

Unfortunately the human became too confident, dropped his guard and was subsequently captured. He has not been heard from since.

With regards to the S.H.S. their record has been truly dismal.

In the six months since the launch of the Special Hog Service the information received back has been minimal, furthermore those who sent it have disappeared off the face of the Earth.

A very disappointed and deeply concerned Air Commodore shook his head. 'There is something sadly wrong and we need to get it sorted, and quickly!'

Nothing more was said, Jeremy Ridgeback, escorted his friend from the Control Sty, bid him farewell and then returned to the rest of his team deep below the earth. As for the Air Commodore, he had one more task to perform and that was a tour of the station.

Despite having learned firsthand of the setback, he still found things to be encouraged about. He was highly impressed by the action above ground, after all RAF Piggin Hill was a top, if not the top, fighter station in the whole of the United Kingdom.

Thanks to the pilots of the aircraft and the backup teams supporting them, Great Britain still remained invasion free. Ask any military expert and they will list a number of requirements needed to win a war, quality personnel, good organisation, great ability and the right equipment.

Then add one vital ingredient, intelligent information as to what the enemy is doing and planning. Without it, it could spell serious trouble.

CHAPTER 2

The French Connection

It was late afternoon and relatively quiet, the silence broken occasionally by a motor vehicle trundling along the cobbled street. Close to the cafe where Madamoiselle Tranches was sitting, an old accordion player swayed forwards and backwards in time to her own music. On the ground, a hat was stragetically placed to attract passersby. It obviously worked, as a small quantity of coins had found their way in and around the old piece of headwear.

'Madamoiselle Tranches?'

The young and rather attractive looking pig turned round.

'Pardon,' she asked quietly.

'The day is for the living,' was the seemingly strange response.

'Monsieur Morceau?'

'Oui je m'appelle Maurice Morceau.'

The couple had never met before but knew of each other's reputation. Both were very respected members of the French Resistance and were doing admirable work for the war effort.

'Ah Monsieur Morceau, I am so pleased to meet you at last.'

The older pig took the young one's front trotter and kissed it gently. 'Call me Maurice.' He smiled.

'And I am Petite, it is my name, not my stature.' She chuckled.

'Ha, Petite how lovely to meet you. It is as if I have known you for such a long time.' This time he moved nearer and confirmed his pleasure by kissing the young attractive pig on both cheeks.

Petite smiled broadly. 'Maurice, I feel exactly the same and this way is so much better than our usual morse code conversation.'

They both nodded in total agreement.

Maurice Morceau was a tailor by trade. His late Grandfather started the business, which he was now running, and had come to France from just over the border many years ago. As a result, Maurice was half French and half German.

Petite on the other hand was one hundred per cent French and hated the Germans for what they had done to her mother and father.

'Would you like something to eat and drink?' Monsieur

Morceau enquired, knowing his young compatriot had probably not eaten properly for days.

'Thank you, you are most kind.'

There was no menu, either food or wine. The cafe offered one thing and one thing only.

The old pig called out to a nearby waiter, 'two bowls please if you would be so kind.'

The waiter nodded. 'Certainement Monsieur, toute de suite!'

One would normally think that Maurice would not want to get involved in anti-German activities, especially as he was half German by birth. Unbeknown to the others, though, he had good reason to dislike those over the border. Like Petite, the Germans had subjected his parents to things he didn't like to repeat, just because they lived in France.

After a short time, the waiter appeared carrying two large tin bowls filled with the usual dish of the day, chunks of raw potatoes, apples and carrots mixed with a cheap dry red wine. Considering it was war time, the French still enjoyed a good selection of food as this showed.

Maurice watched as the young pig sitting opposite enjoyed her welcome meal, both of them not knowing when the next chance to eat might be.

Members of the French Resistance came from all walks of life but they all had the same aim, which was to cause as much mayhem amongst their country's invaders as they could. They were also a special link between the Special Forces, which operated behind enemy lines, and its headquarters back in the United Kingdom.

All information was gathered and relayed by various means, including a small band of very brave pigs known as "The Go Betweens." Petite Tranches and Maurice Morceau were two such members. To be discovered would result in certain death but in their eyes it was a risk worth taking.

For the past six months or so, an enormous effort had been made to delay any progress by the enemy, and this took all forms of action. One of the most effective being undertaken was by a special Truffle unit consisting of about twenty young and very able pigs.

Petite could report on their progress as she followed them on many of their missions. They were very efficient in what they did and it is worth reflecting on one such mission which set the enemy's advance back by many weeks.

Petite Tranches, herself very brave, accompanied her colleagues on a particular evening back in May of this year. Information came through that a large ammunition train was due to make a delivery to an enemy store depot a mere four miles from the front line. Should this have succeeded in getting through, it would have caused serious problems for those trying to stem any advance, so obviously something had to be done.

Working in close collaboration with the Special Forces behind enemy lines and using gathered intelligence, the Truffle unit could pin point the exact route the train would take. All that remained was to work out the best way to stop the consignment getting through.

Before the war Petite had no idea what a truffle was, let alone a Truffle unit. In war, however, one learns very fast.

Each and every member of the Truffle unit had one skill in particular and that was the very efficient use of their snouts! Used to search for truffles, a very expensive commodity found underground, they could dig at an electrifying pace. As a result, and with specialised training, the Truffle unit became very efficient in digging up anything that stood in their way.

Imagine a large tree standing beside a railway bridge and twenty snouts digging as one beneath the roots. It was inevitable that, in a short time, the tree would topple on to the bridge and block anything that was trying to get through.

That is precisely what happened that particular evening in May. Of course the timing had to be right. Blocking the bridge too soon could result in it being discovered and allow time for the train to be diverted. Wait too long and the train would pass the spot before the tree was toppled.

Petite watched and listened intently as the leader of the unit issued his instructions. It was fascinating to see and hear the way the others took in every instruction, knowing that success would bring them their greatest satisfaction in their war effort so far.

Of course, what happened that night is now history and it will go down as one of the most productive missions so far. A complete arsenal destroyed and all due to twenty brave souls, with very strong and efficient snouts, plus Petite of course.

Without vital information and gathered intelligence, as already mentioned, such action could not take place. Just as vital also is information gathered and passed on, outlining the enemy's intention. This can only be gathered and relayed back to the powers that be if the link between those behind enemy lines and the likes of Petite Tranches and Maurice Morceau is not broken.

This was a concern now being shown by the top brass in England and just as much in France. Petite found it so frustrating. She had so very little information to pass on to her resistance colleagues as well as those across the North Sea, in all, it was a very depressing time.

The only reason the train episode came about was due to a chance hearing in a cafe by a resistance member, nothing to do with any intelligence unit. They couldn't be traced, so it was passed on to the special forces by one of Petite's colleagues.

With the sound of the accordion still ringing in their ears, Petite and Maurice sipped their swill cocktail, the juices at the bottom of the tin bowl, and spent the next few moments enjoying each other's company.

It was quite normal to find couples of differing ages seated at pavement cafes so no one would cause to question the nature of their meeting. Perhaps they were father and daughter, uncle or niece or even tutor and pupil. The one thing is they didn't look out of place, and their occasional outburst of laughter would dispel any sinister thoughts amongst those around them. Surely they were just an ordinary couple enjoying a meal and a drink together.

'Well Petite my dear,' Maurice spoke quietly, 'as much as I would like to stay here forever, I am afraid I must get back to the shop.'

'I understand Maurice,' the young pig responded. 'It is time for me to go also.'

'Shall we say one week from now at the Cafe Jardin?' Maurice suggested.

'That will be fine, I look forward to seeing you there.'

The couple finished the contents of their bowls, shook trotters and then walked off in different directions.

At the corner of the street, Petite turned, just in time to see Maurice walk past the accordion player and drop a contribution into the hat. Another job done she thought as she disappeared out of sight.

Was that just an ordinary accordion player? And what about a change of venue for the next meeting, could it be something to do with the link? I wonder.

CHAPTER 3

T'Lad from Barnsley

"Michael Porkinson turn round and pay attention, if you filled your head with as much knowledge as you have Cricket know-how, you would be an academic by now."

Those words still rang loudly in the lad from Barnsley's ears. Michael, or Porky as he was known, remembered what Mr Brown, his old English teacher had said, and for some reason he wished he had taken notice and paid more attention.

Still, working in Spud & Company's Potato Mash manufacturing factory had its compensation. Where else could you spend all day ogling at some of Barnsley's young beauties, whilst at the same time trying to catch up with that education? Having squandered the opportunity to learn at school, Porky now wanted to make amends.

Mashed potato during the Second World War was almost as important as guns and bullets, simply because without food in the belly it meant weakness in the body and no strength to fight. Nourishment was so important.

SPUD & CO'S
POTATO MASH MANUFACTURERS

Of course no one on the noisy production line at Spud & Company gave much thought to that. To them it was a mundane job in a "reet din" of a place. Or more plainly, boring work and a heck of a lot of noise to go with it!

Actually, young Porkinson didn't mind the noise. The thick flaps on the old leather helmet his granddad gave him eliminated any sound, and the books he read whilst operating the various levers on the "spludge plunger" allowed him to enter a world of his own.

With no chance of holding a conversation with anyone, due to the deafening noise from the various machines producing the staple diet of the warring country, the young pig spent his working day looking and reading.

At the time, Michael Porkinson gave no thought to the hours spent at Spud & Co but, unknown to him, it would have an enormous influence on him in the future. This, however, was a long way off.

Granddad Porkinson used to sit his young grandson on his knee and tell him tales of the time he was in the Royal Pig Flying Corps in the First World War. How he became a prisoner when the wooden aircraft he was piloting developed engine trouble and he had to make a forced landing amongst the enemy.

To a young pig it was fascinating to listen to, especially as his granddad made it sound so real, just as if it was happening there and then. Porky heard how he learned to speak German

21

whilst he was held captive and spent a lot of time mimicking his captors.

It really was a fun time sitting, listening to the experiences of the old pig, and Porky would giggle as his granddad spluttered out word by word of German. Of course he had no idea what it meant, but he just loved the language, so much so he persuaded his granddad to teach him lots of the words.

Ironically, when Porky started school, and right through the whole of his school life, the only two things he excelled at were Cricket and German, neither of which would help towards an academic career. There's not a lot of call for German in Barnsley and cricket for pigs was out of the question as far as a career was concerned.

When the history books are written they will show that not only the knowledge of German would play a big part in Porky's life but the game of cricket would also picture rather strongly. There were also a couple of items that would also play a part in the young pig's future, a couple of hand me downs given by Granddad Porkinson to his grandson, namely the leather flying helmet and a pair of goggles used during his days in the Royal Pig Flying Corps.

In the early days of flight there were no such luxuries as covered in cockpits and any flying was open to the elements. The helmet, therefore, kept the head protected and warm, whereas the goggles played a big part in protecting the eyes from objects that may whizz by at any given moment. They were, therefore, two valuable pieces of gear.

Not only that but they became a big talking point whenever friends popped round to Porky's to see him. Whoever it was visiting couldn't resist trying both items on and "flying" an imaginary mission against the famous German fighter ace "The Red Bacon".

After each sortie, the goggles found their way on the shelf ready for the next visitors. The helmet on the other hand became an integral part of Porky's attire. He wore it all the time and the question was asked if he actually slept in it. A reply was never forthcoming.

Michael Porkinson had a happy piglethood, even though life was hard. He was the youngest of a litter of six, brought up by his grandparents soon after he was born. No one really knew what happened to his parents but rumour was rife that a human called Farmer Thomson had taken the couple away to a building called an abattoir, whatever that was.

Porky's home, that of his grandparents, was a terraced sty just on the outskirts of Barsnley, next to a large coalfield. A small stream ran by, which could prove very useful after a day spent slag boarding down large heaps of coal waste. Slag boarding was a sport introduced a long time ago by a fellow pig and it proved to be one of the most popular sports in the pig world. It was, as you can imagine, a dirty activity, so the passing stream was a huge bonus.

At any one time, twenty or so pigs could be seen splashing around in the clear water after a day's boarding and gradually changing from a dirty black colour back to their natural bright pink.

There was nothing more fun than whizzing down a slippery heap of coal slag and finishing ahead of the competition. To be champion slag boarder of Barnsley was a prestigious title and Porky was proud to claim it.

'Have you had a good day Porky?' his grandmother enquired as he walked through the sty door'

'Yes thank you Gran,' he replied. 'It was reet good fun.'

Granny and Granddad Porkinson, now rather old, spent most of their time inside the sty and had no idea what their grandson had been up to. He always came home spotless so they assumed he had been with friends playing chess or some other tranquil activity. Anything else and surely he would come home filthy like they used to do when they were small. If only they had known!

Pigs grow up much quicker than humans and it wasn't long before Porky outgrew his slag boarding days. Unfortunately, though, there wasn't a lot for older pigs to do in and around Barnsley, and he never did fancy hanging about on street corners like his mates. Instead he became a bit of a loner.

'How is that?' a loud cry echoed around the area where Porky was walking along the banks of the stream.

'Whatever was that?' the lone pig said to himself, looking in the direction where the noise had come from. 'Sounded like some of those humans.'

Porky clambered up the steep bank beside the stream, and came across a large expanse of grass. He was confronted by a strange sight, humans dressed all in white dotted about everywhere with two of them carrying pieces of wood, and one of them trying to hit a red ball.

It seemed ridiculous that the game, which was obviously cricket, had not been heard of in the pig world, but on the other hand did humans know of slag boarding?

For the next few hours or so, Porky was fascinated by what he saw from his vantage point. Making mental notes of what was happening, he realised there was life after slag boarding and it was he who was responsible for introducing the game of cricket to pigs all over the county. In fact it soon caught on and pig cricketers were soon playing the game all over the world.

Of course, being built as pigs were, they would never be able to compete with the humans at the game, but that wouldn't stop them from holding their own competitions. Nor would it stop them from introducing rules that would allow for easier play. For example, a pig found it very difficult to bowl overarm therefore under trotter bowling was introduced. Whatever the game became it would be very competitive because that is pigs' nature.

Porky was a very lucky pig, he had experienced slag boarding at a high level, and introduced and played pig cricket. He was also fortunate in as much as he had a vivid imagination.

When not playing his version of cricket, he would journey

along the stream to watch the humans. There he would simply close his eyes and in no time his imagination would take over.

'Now then Porky, I want you to go out there and show them what you can do.'

It was the captain of Yorkshire County Cricket Club.

'I'll do my best captain,' Porky replied having padded up and now making his way to the middle.

All of a sudden a loud rushing noise brought Porky back to reality. It was the sound of one of the fielders who almost collided with the young pig as he attempted to retrieve a ball hit to the boundary. Porky made a quick exit, thinking that perhaps human cricket fields aren't the place for pigs to be.

It didn't stop him daydreaming though. When he should have been learning or carrying out some other task, Porky was often in his own world, helping Yorkshire towards the title or even almost single handed regaining the ashes for England.

'As I have said before Porkinson, you'll never make anything of yourself if you don't start concentrating on learning.'

In truth, Porky probably never heard a word the teacher had just uttered, it was more likely his mind was on some cricket field somewhere.

As we all know, unless you are exceptional, a living cannot be made out of cricket, and certainly not in the pig world.

Professional slag boarding was also a non-entity.

Apart from a small amount of a foreign language and a great amount of cricket knowledge, Porky had little else to show for his time at school. It was hardly any surprise, then, that the daydreaming pig would finish up as a machine operator at the local mashed potato manufacturing company.

In times of war, it was a case of all hands to the mill. Those who were able volunteered to fight for King and country. There were, however, many who also proved essential to the war effort. Miners, farm workers, Doctors, Nurses and many more, including those that helped to provide food for a hungry nation.

Porky would rather be fighting on the front line than working in a factory, but as he was too young he had no choice. The only consolation was that, had he been overseas fighting, he would probably have not met the love of his life, Alice Swizzell.

Alice was one of the bevvy of beauties on the production line at the factory. It was her shy smile that first attracted Porky to her, plus the way she blushed when he winked as their eyes met across the floor.

Porky himself was rather shy but there was no way he was going to miss the opportunity of getting to know young Alice better.

'How about a drink after work?' Porky mouthed.

Alice smiled and nodded. 'Seven o'clock?'

Thank goodness they could both lip read as it was impossible to hear what had been said above the noise of the machines.

And so it was. Porky had found his true love.

Whenever the opportunity arose the two youngsters could be found enjoying a bowl of lemonade at the local "The Human and Whistle".

'When do you think the war will end Porky?' Alice would ask as they cuddled up to each other.

'No idea Alice,' the young pig replied. 'No idea.'

And the truth is no one anywhere knew the answer. It could be weeks, it could be months, and, perish the thought, it could be years.

CHAPTER 4

Pigs Will Fly!

Drive through Lincolnshire in the thirties or forties and there was a good chance you would come across an airfield. Look up to the sky and there was even a bigger chance you would see a large aircraft. These would be either going on a bombing mission over Germany or returning from one, having deposited their bombs on some factory site, or perhaps a dam or two.

One such airfield in the county was RAF Spampton, a very important airfield indeed.

'Right, you horrible lot, stand by your straw!'

A rather tall, heavily built figure was standing in the doorway of the billet for new recruits. It was Sergeant Sidebottom, loved, it was said, by only his mother.

'I want you lot outside in five minutes,' the Sergeant howled. 'And the last one out will be put on billet cleaning duty.'

It takes very little imagination to work out what that involved.

RAF Spampton was something rather special. Yes it did have the usual fleet of Avro Lancaster bombers, but one of them had been adapted for secret and important missions.

'Now listen for your names,' Sergeant Sidebottom shouted, as the last recruit appeared from inside the billet.

'Snoutcliffe, Hockley, Salter.'

'Here! Sarg,' they all responded.

'Right,' the Sergeant turned to face the others, 'the rest of you report to number three hangar – you three follow me!'

As the bulk of the recruits marched off towards the designated hangar, Sergeant Sidebottom headed off at speed in the opposite direction, closely followed by the three selected pigs.

After a walk, or more accurate, a forced trek, the four came across a door marked "Top Secret – Knock and Wait".

The Sergeant stepped up to the door and gave it a loud rap with the stick he always carried. In a short time, the hinge on a small spy hole moved and an eye appeared.

'Sidebottom,' the Sergeant called out. The eye moved first to the left and then to the right. Then, satisfied, the door opened and all four stepped inside.

It was a rather suave gentlepig seated at a large wooden desk who greeted his visitors. 'Welcome to "Operation Pigs will Fly",' he said rather proudly.

The three recruits looked at each other, all somewhat bewildered by the greeting.

'Keep your eyes to the front!' Sergeant Sidebottom screamed at the top of his voice.

'That's alright Sergeant, it's just a natural reaction,' the older gentlepig said quietly, as he rose to his trotters.

It was obvious the older pig had been an officer for some time as the row of medals on his uniform confirmed.

'Now come and sit over here,' he indicated, 'and I will explain what this is all about. Then I am sure you will appreciate just how much the world is relying on you.'

Over the next hour or so, a clear picture would emerge, and the three young recruits would learn, firstly what the S.H.S.(Special Hog Service) was all about, and secondly, what their duties would involve.

To begin with, all three would learn parachuting, something pigs didn't normally come across. They would also learn the art of lip reading and, finally, a good grasp of the German language.

It would be the task of the pigs to find out what the enemy was planning, by getting close up to their operational headquarters. Once the information had been gathered, it would be relayed to a member of the French Resistance, who in turn would transfer it by various means back to the Intelligence Unit based in the United Kingdom. Obviously the task would be highly dangerous, but, if they succeeded, it would be so rewarding.

Lincolnshire, already known as Bomber County, would also become known as Bicycle County. The reason being that most of it is as flat as a pancake and many people found a bicycle was an ideal mode of transport, especially with fuel being rationed and in short supply. It was also ideal to learn parachuting.

Now it must be appreciated that parachuting can only take place if the partaker is flying, something somewhat alien to the pig community. All three recruits were now wondering what they were getting themselves into. They wouldn't have long to wait for the answer.

Somewhat scared, but at the same time excited, the selected three had over the next few months taken their first flight, parachuted from an aircraft, learned to lip read and had managed to grasp a good understanding of the German language. The Special Hog Service had gained three very worthy and competent members.

In a short time, all three would be on their way across the water and dropped behind enemy lines. All that was left was for the wheels of intelligence gathering to be put in motion and the information gathered and scrutinised.

Petite Tranche, the pretty young French Resistance fighter had already been briefed to expect the airdrop of the three S.H.S members. Her job was to make contact with them as soon as possible. This alone was very risky, to do this she had to get behind enemy lines, lay low and then wait for the drop.

It was late afternoon when the Lancaster Bomber took off from RAF Spampton. In a few hours it would hopefully be over France and in a position to deposit its special load. Inside, the three pigs were experiencing various emotions, they were very scared, very cold but at the same time very excited.

'Stand by! Stand by!' the voice over the intercom crackled into life and although expected it still came as a shock to the three passengers. One by one they shuffled to the drop hatch.

'This is it,' one of them yelled. 'Good luck, good luck!'

And so the time came, in turn the young pigs eased into position just above the hatch, eventually slipping out into the cold air. They were on their way.

It was up to the rear gunner to advise the pilot that all were clear and all parachutes had been deployed. He watched the three pigs for a time before announcing, 'all safely deposited, all parachutes opened, let's go home skipper!'

With that, the large bomber banked sharply to the left, manoeuvred a full turn and headed back to the relative safety of RAF Spampton.

It took quite a time for the three parachutists to reach the ground, but reach it they did, all safely landing in one piece. As far as they could make out, the three of them would have landed within a mile of each other so the next task was to gather up their parachutes and rendezvous at the earliest possible moment.

Having said all this, there was quite a bit of enemy activity in the area and with instructions not to take unnecessary risks, they decided to lay low for a while. A captured S.H.S member is of no use to anyone except, of course, the Germans.

The parachute drop could be described as being very accurate because, miraculously, Petite Tranches saw it unfold right before her eyes. It was bright moonlight when the aircraft came into view and the young resistance fighter watched in awe as the three pigs descended beneath their silk canopies.

One after the other, Petite saw them drop to the ground, the nearest one only some hundred yards from where she was hiding in the undergrowth. She wondered if she had been the only one to see the spectacle, or would other eyes have seen it?

Fortunately her fears were unfounded as she was able to witness the pig nearest to her taking cover as soon as possible.

It was tempting for Petite to make herself known there and then but, being aware of a tiring flight, she decided all three should be allowed to rest. A few more hours wouldn't make any difference and, in any case, she herself would benefit from a good sleep. For that reason the young resistance fighter settled down in anticipation of an interesting venture which lay ahead of her the next morning.

No more than an hour had passed when Petite suddenly shot up with a start! Coming towards her were the sound of lots of footsteps and worse, German voices.

'Oh no, no,' she said to herself. 'Be quiet, please, please be quiet.'

Suddenly the young fighter felt her heart pounding and for a very good reason. About a hundred yards from where she was she could hear a loud sound. She couldn't believe it, it was the sound of a pig GRUNTING!

'Franz! Over here,' a German voice called out across the waste land. 'I think we have another English Pig!'

There was nothing that could have been done, a large number of the enemy forces came running and surrounded the spot where the sound had come from.

'On your trotters, English Pig,' one of the soldiers demanded.

Young Petite, trembling with fear, watched helplessly as the S.H.S member was pighandled and bundled into a vehicle which had just drawn up.

'Not a bad evening's work,' the driver called back to his colleagues. 'Three English Pigs in one night, pretty good going Ja?'

The vehicle moved off, the soldiers moved away and the young Petite sat stunned, reflecting on what had just happened.

CHAPTER 5

Somewhere Out There

Lord Hamilton Hogsby was a prominent figure in the industrial world. His interests included two large farms, a munitions factory near Middlesbrough and his favourite business, Spud & Company.

Situated a few miles from Sheffield, Lord Hogsby ran his empire from Quaqmire Hall, his ancestral home. Not any ordinary home though, because within the grounds lay the biggest complex of defence systems in the whole of Europe. Not only that but within the complex was housed countless top figures of the pig world.

The "Warren", as the complex was known, included sophisticated communication devices, workshops, education establishments and a top of the range medical centre. All financed from the profits of Lord Hogsby's empire.

In addition to all this was a spray shop, one of those places where vehicles went to be painted after they had been damaged. What possible use could a place like that be, this was a Ministry of Defence establishment not a commercial vehicle painting centre?

Back at the main hall it was to be an evening of great importance, Quagmire Hall would welcome the majority, if not all, of the most prominent people to date associated with the war effort.

Air Commodore Sir Norman Thyne-Rashers, Wing Commander Jeremy Ridgeback, and most of the high ranking personnel from Fighter and Bomber Command were present. Add a number of important Cabinet Ministers and it was obvious just how important the gathering would be.

In the Great Hall, an impressive table had been set. The candles flickered, sending shadows dancing across the walls and ceiling, which added to the ambience and enabled the guests to move their thoughts away from the war, if only for a short period of time.

Lord Hogsby, most suitably attired for such an important evening held an elegant looking phone to his ear and, using his free trotter, rotated the handle vigorously. 'Gilbert, Hogsby here. Is everything in order?'

The manager in charge of the hall, Askew Gilbert, reassured the Lord, 'the temporary staff arrived an hour ago and we will be ready to serve in less than ten minutes.'

There was a big advantage owning a business. The number of personnel at ones disposal was always more than adequate. This time Lord Hogsby had chosen Spud & Company as the supplier of temporary staff on this particular night.

'It makes a change not having to lip read,' Porky said quietly.

'You're absolutely right,' Alice agreed, with a sweet smile.

It wasn't quite the same as enjoying a drink at the Human and Whistle, or indeed looking at each other across the factory floor, but at least they were together. Both Porky and Alice had been chosen as members of the temporary staff employed for the special evening.

'Right it's time to serve the drinks,' a voice called out from the hall.

Porky immediately collected his tray and made his way into the large reception hall where the Lord's guests were waiting, Alice, for her part, entered the kitchen in readiness for her duties.

Porky remembered the first time he had been involved in one of Lord Hogsby's evenings. It was nerve racking, all that top brass and the other important people, but now it was second nature to him.

'A little bird tells me you like cricket?' a rather smart dressed guest announced as he sidled up to the young waiter.

'Yes sir,' Porky replied,'love to watch it, but not very good at playing the game.'

'Me too, a fascinating game though. It's a lot like war.'

The young pig was not sure what the guest meant but then realised what he was referring to when he went on to explain.

'It's like war in as much as you try to beat the enemy by knocking six bells out of them!'The guest then gave out a huge guffaw as if it was the comment of the century.

Porky had no idea who he was talking to, but in politeness he gave a big smile. It was amazing, here was a young working class pig talking on the same level as people way above his station, who would ever have imagined that? With a satisfied expression, Porky moved on.

His young Alice looked so sweet with a black apron draped around her shapely body, her white blouse showing off the rest of her slender figure. Porky looked across the hall as she entered carrying her tray and felt such a lucky pig.

'I love you,' he mouthed as she looked across at him.

Alice blushed slightly and turned away with the same smile that occurred that time at the factory.

Over the next hour or so the guests had been fed and watered. Now they had retired to the large billiard room for after dinner drinks and probably a catch up with all the gossip.

This allowed Porky and Alice the opportunity to slip away and have a bit of time together.

'Quickly in here,' Porky whispered, making sure at first it was all clear. 'We'll be safe in here and no one will disturb us.'

Alice followed Porky into what turned out to be Lord Hogsby's study. A very large room adorned by plush leather furniture with long draped curtains at the windows. A large oak desk sat prominently beneath a picture of Quagmire Hall. A grand piano in a far corner completed the furnishings.

'I don't feel very safe in here,' Alice squeaked rather nervously.

Porky tried to reassure her, 'Don't worry sweetheart, we'll be alright. If we hear anyone coming it's just a matter of nipping behind the piano and waiting until they've gone.'

Call it fate or whatever you like but no sooner had Porky finished reassuring his young love, voices were heard outside the study.

Like a flash the two of them shot across the floor and squeezed behind the piano. 'We must keep absolutely quiet,' Porky said, stating the obvious. This is a rather difficult thing for pigs to do, however, because by nature they do tend to make the odd noise without realising it.

The door creaked open. 'I won't be long,' a voice uttered above the sound of the footsteps on the bare floor. 'Make yourself comfortable and I will brief you as to what has occurred.'

The two pigs behind the piano listened intently as it was obvious that an important meeting was about to take place.

'I think you all know each other,' an authoritative voice announced, 'but with the possible exception of our distinguished visitor Madame Nicole. Mme Nicole is a very important member of the French Resistance.'

All at once loud applause rang round the room because everyone present, except Porky and Alice of course, recognised her as the "Accordian Woman" one of the main links between them and the lads dropped behind enemy lines. Madame Nicole paid frequent visits to the UK, but this was the first time she had been present at such a high profile meeting.

'Monsieurs,' Mme Nicole began, 'as you know we rely on your brave pigs to feed us information so we in turn can get it back to you. Alas I have some very grave news!'

Whilst neither Porky nor Alice could see what was going on they sensed great tension in the room.

As they waited and listened Porky recognised the next voice as that belonging to Wing Commander Jeremy Ridgeback, who he had served drinks to earlier.

'Grave news?' the Wing Commander asked.

'I am afraid so,' Mme Nicole replied. 'I have to report that your latest operation resulted in all of the members of the Special Hog Service being captured only minutes after landing.'

It was Sir Norman Thyne-Rasher's turn to ask a question.

43

'Have you any indication as to why they were captured, and so early on?'

'Yes, Sir Norman,' the French guest replied, 'and it is thanks to one of my fellow country pigs, Madamoiselle Petite Tranches, and her bravery, that we know exactly why all of the S.H.S members were captured so quickly.'

There was a pause before Mme Nicole responded, 'It is Gentlepigs, because of uncontrollable grunting!'

During the day, or anytime a pig is awake, he or she can control their grunts. When they are asleep it is a different matter. It is similar to humans and their snoring.

How many times have humans denied they snored when clearly it has been proven in fact they do snore? It is the same with pigs, when asleep they don't know if they grunt or not. Clearly they do and it is because of this their whereabouts are detected.

Lord Hogsby the last person to arrive at the meeting found it all disturbing and began to pace up and down. 'Does it mean the end of operations?'

'It will be only temporary,' the Air Commodore said reassuringly. 'We have the means here to rectify the problem, and do it we shall!'

'Bravo Sir Norman. That is the spirit,' Madame Nicole called out. 'It is vital that you solve the problem so you can help us to drive the enemy from our beloved country.'

'Now Gentlefriends, if you will excuse me I have a long trip back home across the water to continue the fight, I therefore bid you all au revoir monsieurs, au revoir.'

With that the French Resistance member turned and made her way to the door.

Mme Nicole added, as she walked out, 'What you have just said Sir Norman will help me to reassure my country that the British will succeed.'

She closed the door behind her and the people in the room listened as her footsteps gradually grew weaker and weaker.

'Have you any ideas Air Commodore?' Lord Hogsby enquired.

Sir Norman nodded affirmatively. 'I do have something in mind but it is going to be a very brave pig to take it on.'

Turning to his colleague Jeremy Ridgeback he asked, 'Who is available from the Special Hog Service?'

'I'm not sure,' the Wing Commander answered. 'What did you mean by a very brave pig to take it on?'

'I can't really say at the moment,' Sir Norman responded. 'But let's say if you have the names of anyone you think could fit the bill jot it down on that notepad on the piano and I will pick it up before I leave this evening. Now let's get back to the social gathering, it may be the last for some time.'

Before leaving the room each member present approached the piano to offer their suggestions. Soon they had all left and it was time for Porky and Alice to make their exit.

'You go first Alice,' Porky suggested. 'And I will follow.'

Young Alice Swizzell crept very gently to the door, opened it, and carefully checked no one was about. As soon as she was satisfied it was all clear, she slipped away to join the other temporary staff in the kitchen. She did, however, become somewhat agitated when a considerable time elapsed and there was still no sign of Porky. Had he been caught, she wondered.

'Ha there you are,' a relieved Alice called out when Porky emerged. 'Where on earth have you been?'

Porky smiled, 'I haven't been anywhere,' he replied. 'I just wanted to see who the brave pigs are around here!'

CHAPTER 6

Full of Surprises

After the events of the weekend, Porky and Alice were soon back to making eyes at each other again across the factory floor at Spud & Company. The rest of the manufacturing unit was operating as usual, potatoes going in at one end and mash coming out the other with various stages of production in between.

Along the line, a tall authoritative figure strolled at a steady pace until he came to where Porky was stationed.

'Someone needs to see you at the office,' the pig, who was the manager of the factory said, brushing down his white coat as if it was being attacked by potato mash.

Porky had turned the moment the manager reached him and was able to read his lips.

Porky in turn mouthed a question, 'Do you mean right now?' he asked.

'Yes, I will take over until you return.'

48

The young pig left his machine in the capable trotters of his manager and made his way to the office. Like many factories, the office was up a flight of steps which took Porky a little longer than usual to reach. As soon as he reached his destination, he knocked and waited. Through the glass in the door Porky recognised a number of pigs he had seen at Quagmire Hall.

'Come in young pig,' a voice called out.

Porky obeyed the command and walked in. He began to feel a little nervous.

'Porkinson, your name has appeared on a list of very brave pigs, any reason why that is?'

The pig asking the question was none other than Lord Hogsby.

'Er! Well!' Porky stuttered, 'I am not sure.'

Lord Hogsby stood up and walked over to Porky. He then shook the young pig vigorously by the trotter.

'Well, whatever the reason, you are the chosen one,' the Lord announced proudly. 'He is one of mine,' he added turning to the others in the office, expressing delight as if Porky had just won a major race or something.

'Are you sure it's me Lord Hogsby?' Porky asked, wanting confirmation.

'I am absolutely positive,' the titled gentlepig and factory owner replied. 'When the others on the list found out what was involved they backed out, couldn't stomach it, not like a Spud & Co worker. Good show Porky!'

Porky began to shake nervously. What had he done by adding his name to that list in the study?

Lord Hogsby then went on to add, 'Of course the others thought you might be too young but I dismissed this, I said if you worked for me you would be more than capable.'

Porky, still shaking, asked in a rather feeble squeak. 'The others what others?'

'The Air Commodore and the Wing Commander, but don't worry I have convinced them you are the right pig for the job.

In two days time Porky would have to say goodbye to his beloved Alice, tell his relations he was going away for some time and bid farewell to his mates at the Human and Whistle.

He would never forget Alice's reaction when he told her of his sudden departure.

'I just felt I needed to do something,' he said, gently holding her trotter.

'So you just added your name to a list without giving any thought to what was really involved.' By her tone Porky could sense that Alice was very concerned.

'I just had to do it,' Porky explained. 'Please don't be angry, I thought by doing this I would make something of myself.'

Alice snuggled up close. 'I am not angry,' she said. 'If anything I am so proud of you, but you don't have to make something of yourself, you are already something to me, and I am going to miss you.'

Porky felt somewhat humbled by Alice's words, 'I hope you will miss me,' he said, 'because I am certainly going to miss you. You will wait for me won't you?'

Alice put both of her trotters round Porky and gave him a kiss he would remember throughout his venture. 'Of course I will wait for you,' Alice whispered. 'Forever if it takes that amount of time!'

Porky reported to Quagmire Hall, except this time it was to the complex and not the elegant building he had visited previously. Soon things would become very serious and, to be revealed a little later, very dangerous.

The young pig, however, was confident he was up to the task whatever it was, even though he was not sure exactly what was involved.

Porky had made his way along a main corridor in search of room seventeen, the number he had been instructed to report to.

When he eventually found the room he noticed it wasn't any

different from any of the others along the way, the same white walls and the same sturdy brown door. Inside, not a lot of difference either.

The pig sitting behind a desk looked no different from any other pig he had met, except this one was wearing a white coat, probably indicating a medical pig. No doubt the explanation offered would make everything clear.

'Just before I explain things,' the white coat clad pig said. 'I would like to introduce myself. I am Doctor Barnes Scratchings. Now sit yourself down and I will fill you in as to what we have in store for you.'

Porky sat down and listened intently. The word operation came up frequently in the doctor's explanation, which was understandable when military personnel were involved in such things. What Porky found a little disturbing though, was that the word operation didn't always refer to a military one. This became quite clear when in the final sentence the doctor suggested Porky would only be hospitalised for a week or so!

This was a huge shock to the system, Porky jolted upright, or as upright as a pig can be. 'Hospitalised?' he enquired.

'Yes,' the doctor answered. 'Were you not told of this when you were accepted for the job?'

It was now becoming a little complicated. If Porky answered negatively the doctor would want to know why, and that could, as they say, open up a can of worms. The inevitable question of who put his name on the list would come up and who knows where it would go from there.

What was the sentence for listening in on a top brass secret meeting, and then putting one's own name on a list of such importance?

Porky nodded and answered, 'Oh, the operation, hospitalised, yes, yes. I remember now.'

'Now you will want to know what is really involved,' Doctor Scratchings began. 'When Sir Norman came up with his idea my team thought it would be impossible, after all, it is only natural for us pigs to grunt, especially when we are asleep. To stop us grunting is like attempting to stop humans from snoring, almost impossible without cutting out the voice box!'

Porky almost fainted when he heard the doctor utter the words he had just done.

'But don't worry,' Doctor Scratchings spoke reassuringly. 'We are not going to do that, after all what use is a pig without a voice box?'

A huge sigh of relief filled the room and Porky's body began to regain the pink complexion which had drained away seconds earlier.

Doctor Scratchings referred to his team, which was made up of many pigs with varying talents. Some in fact were multi talented and none more so than Doctor Scratchings, who himself was an inventor, an engineer, a chemist and a painter.

When the Air Commodore came up with his suggestion to stop grunting and therefore avoid capture, they all set to work. The doctor, for his part, was confident they had come up with the answer. It was however going to be tricky. The operation to be carried out had never been done before and was therefore classed as pioneer surgery. Furthermore, it wouldn't be known if it had been a success until some days later.

Doctor Barnes Scratchings had almost finished explaining everything when a loud knock occurred.

The doctor responded by calling out, 'Come in.'

The door opened gently to reveal yet another pig, dressed very similar to Dr Scratchings, white coat with the addition of a pair of glasses balanced on the end of his snout. There were also a number of items protruding from a pocket. His appearance was that of another inventor.

As he entered the room, Porky noticed a small box in his right trotter which he was holding up for the benefit of Doctor Scratchings.

'Ah, you have it Chippo, well done!'

The older pig trundled in and handed it over. 'Brilliant,' Doctor Scratchings said enthusiastically. 'This could be the answer.'

'Oh I am sorry,' the doctor apologised. 'Porky, this is Chippo Bogliss, one of our top and most respected inventors.'

'I am very pleased to meet you Mr Bogliss,' Porky said, holding out a trotter.

'Well this is what is going to help us win the war,' Doctor Scratchings gleamed as he had a quick peep in the box.

'Well it certainly should help.'

Porky watched on with great interest. How could such a small thing go such a long way to helping to win the War? What was its purpose anyway? Would he ever learn what it was all about?

Strangely enough, nothing more was mentioned about the

contents of the box, only that what was inside would be known as a V.C.A.G.D. Porky did notice Top Secret stamped in red on the box, so he knew it would be a waste of time asking for an explanation. In any case the least known about secrets, the better, especially if one was unlucky enough to be captured and interrogated under pressure.

The operation, medical type, was due to take place in the next week or so. To take his mind off things, Porky was put to work in other parts of the complex. Rooms five and eleven were significant, the former was a German language classroom and the latter, as indicated on the door, was "Lip reading for advanced users".

For the next few days Porky was to spend equal time in both rooms. Although he had a reasonable knowledge of both, additional learning could only prove beneficial. And so it was to prove!

It was a cold Thursday morning when a pretty young nurse prepared Porky for surgery. 'A lovely body,' he thought, 'but no way as nice as my beautiful Alice.'

'Now this will help you to relax,' the young nurse said softly as Porky lay on the trolley. The sight of a needle usually gave him some cause for concern, but this time he took it in his stride. Perhaps it was because he was thinking of Alice, or the busy time he had spent during the last few days learning more German and perfecting his lip reading. Then, of course, there was the thought of what lay ahead beyond the operation.

'Now, breathe deeply Mr Porkinson,' the nurse said, gently moving the trolley, and then injecting him just above the trotter.

'By the time you count to ten you will be in a nice state of mind.'

Sure enough Porky slipped peacefully into a sleep, still not knowing what the operation was about. It didn't seem to matter now.

It was an absolutely gorgeous summer evening and Headingly cricket ground, home of the Yorkshire County Cricket Club was packed to capacity. It was the final day of the Yorkshire versus Lancashire match, known as the War of the Roses, and always keenly contested with a lot of pride at stake for both sides.

The tension was almost unbearable as the Yorkshire bowler began his long run up to the wicket, knowing that Lancashire needed one run to draw and two to win off this, the last ball of the match.

Half of the huge crowd couldn't bear to watch, while the others sat with their trotters crossed hoping their team would pull off a memorable win.

'Thud! Whack! The batsman swung his bat and caught the ball right in the middle. Like a rocket the ball sped towards the boundary and it looked like a win for the visiting team, Lancashire.

But, wait a second, no one had reckoned on the speed of good old Porky, the first pig ever to be picked for the full human Yorkshire side!

In one motion Porky chased towards the ball, gathered it in his right front trotter and hurled it at the nearest set of wickets. "How's that?" A crescendo of voices rang out as the ball scattered the wicket in all directions.

There was now a long period of silence as everyone fixed their eyes on the umpire. All of a sudden the whole of the cricket ground erupted as the umpire slowly raised a finger to indicate the batsman had been run out and Yorkshire had won. Furthermore, Porky was the hero of the day.

On the pitch every single fielder ran over to Porky and swamped him with hugs and continuous pats on the back. Meanwhile the Yorkshire people in the crowd were almost out of control with joy. This win would be the highlight of the season, nothing was better than beating the old enemy.

After all the team congratulations, the proud pig made his way into the pavilion. He couldn't believe it, there waiting to greet him was his Granny and Granddad, and not only that but many more familiar faces, all his workmates including the girls from Spud and Co. Amazingly there was also Lord Hogsby, Air Commodore Sir Norman Thyne-Rashers and Wing Commander Jeremy Ridgeback, he really couldn't take it all in.

As he made his way back up the pavilion steps everybody started chanting, 'Porky, Porky, Porky.' It was a fantastic feeling and it didn't stop there. As he reached the top of the steps Porky's heart skipped a beat. Standing in the doorway was his lovely sweetheart Alice, looking so radiant and proud.

Walking up to meet the hero she moved close and whispered, 'Well done Mr Porkinson, well done!'

'Mr Porkinson, what does she mean?' he thought. 'She never calls me Mr Porkinson.'

Suddenly Porky realised all was not what it seemed. Gradually his eyes opened and came into focus. Standing over him was the young nurse he had met earlier. 'Mr Porkinson,' she uttered gently. 'Well done, well done, you've come through the operation with flying colours.'

'So it was only a dream,' Porky sighed to himself. 'Ah well not to worry it was nice while it lasted.'

The operation had taken three hours to perform, and the fact that Porky had survived, and the nurse had spoken with such confidence, pointed to a promising outcome. Furthermore, apart from a slight discomfort in the throat, the young pig felt quite good.

Dr Barnes Scratchings, the one who performed the operation, reached for Porky's right front trotter and shook it firmly.

'Well done Porky,' he said with a broad grin, 'an absolute success, both the operation and the result we had hoped to achieve.'

'You know already? Porky quizzed the doctor.

'Oh yes, as soon as the operation was over we knew, didn't we nurse?'

The nurse nodded and smiled, 'Yes straight away.'

Because everything that takes place in the complex was Top Secret, nothing could be revealed.

As far as Porky was concerned there was no difference apart from that slight discomfort, he could talk normally, move his head normally and he felt exactly the same as he had done before the operation. It was becoming a mystery.

Three days had passed since the operation and Porky was moved out of the medical section into an isolation ward. It was so isolated that the young pig never saw or heard anyone other than Doctor Scratchings, and that was only periodically. Food was served via a serving hatch and it was so quiet Porky thought he was in prison. Why the need for all this secrecy?

The ward was quite large for one pig and boasted its own ablutions. Also on the walls, instead of the usual pictures, learning cards were fixed at regular intervals, all with the same subject – German!

With lots of spare time and nothing else to do, Porky soon further improved his grasp of the language.

It was clear from the isolation that the young pig was being prepared for his very important task. There was even more evidence of this when Doctor Scratchings removed a board from the wall to reveal a window.

'Imagine if you will,' the doctor uttered, 'that those two people over there are German soldiers. Take these binoculars and see if you can make out what they are saying.'

The doctor handed over the binoculars and added, 'Today they will speak in English but tomorrow it may be German!'

Although a little nervous, Porky, after having to lip read when he worked at the factory, mastered the task without a problem.

'You really are the best lip reader we have ever had,' Doctor Scratching said pleasingly.

Porky felt very proud and, strangely enough, quite relaxed.

'Shall we say the mission takes place in six weeks time?' the doctor suggested.

Porky just stood in silence.

'Six weeks it is then,' Doctor Barnes Scratchings confirmed.

CHAPTER 7

Put it Down to Pig Error

The Air Commodore's latest visit to Quagmire Hall was such a contrast from the previous one. This time everyone would see a different side to the top ranking pig.

'How on earth could it have happened?' he asked in a very stern tone, demanding an answer.

No one responded. The room remained silent with everyone inside looking at each other.

'Well?' Sir Norman shouted, now becoming somewhat irate. 'Does anyone have the answer?'

It was Doctor Scratchings who eventually stepped forward. 'I think we have to put it down to pig error,' he said somewhat embarrassed.

'Pig error? Pig error?' Sir Norman snapped. 'Do you realise we have all put that young pig in grave danger and at the same time jeopardised the whole operation?'

It was now the turn of the other inventor, Chippo Bogliss, to step forward.

'I am afraid it may have been my fault,' he said apologetically.

'And who are you?'

'It's Chippo Bogliss, Sir Norman, one of our finest inventors.' This time it was Wing Commander Jeremy Ridgeback who nudged forward. 'He is responsible for many of the things used to fight the war.'

Doctor Scratchings added his further comments, 'If it hadn't been for Chippo things could have been worse than they are now.'

There was a feeling that both the doctor and the Wing Commander were trying to diffuse matters and it seemed to work because Sir Norman was gradually becoming less agitated.

'Well what are we going to do about it?' the Air Commodore queried.

The problem had come to light the evening after the operation. Porky had come through it without any problems and being assured everything was fine, he had lay back and waited for the next stage.

Only the operating team knew things were not as they should be and it was after a considerable time that Doctor Scratchings

decided to reveal all. It was so serious that a Top Brass meeting was called.

Remembering that all matters at Quagmire Hall and the Complex were treated as top secret the complete truth could take fifty years to surface. We do know however that the gadget known as V.C.A.G.D was at the head of matters. It was also known that a label attached to it had been switched. Deliberate or by accident we may never know.

We do know however that Porky had been fitted with a device that clearly wasn't the Voice Changing Anti Grunt Device (V.C.A.G.D). It was the same size and shape but it wasn't what it should be.

Inventor Bogliss was now becoming very concerned indeed. If

Porky hadn't been fitted with the correct device, and he certainly hadn't been, were there more mix ups?

In all Chippo Bogliss had prepared more than a dozen of the devices and each, although identical in looks, had different applications. For instance, one helped a human to talk. Another was fitted into a musical instrument to alter the tone, and there were many others.

Of course all the devices had different code names. The P.A.J.S.V.C became the Punch And Judy Special Voice Creator. The Y.G.P.S.S was the Young Girl Pop Star Screamer, which was to be fitted to a Pop Group Fan who had lost her voice and was due to go to a big concert in the near future.

The mystery of the switch, or otherwise, appeared to be easy to solve, find who had been fitted with the one earmarked for Porky and a swap could be made. Admittedly it would delay things but it would be worth it, or would it?

The problem wasn't that easy to solve and regrettably none of this was possible as quite a few of the gadgets had been fitted to recipients who lived in the wild and would be miles away by now.

The only alternative was to explain to Porky what had happened and give him the choice whether to continue or abort the whole operation. Of course everyone knew the answer to that.

It must be remembered that the whole idea for fitting the

V.C.A.G.D was to stop the young pig grunting when he was asleep. It is, as mentioned previously, the same as humans snoring. The sleeper is unaware of any noise being made.

History shows that all pigs captured by the Germans were asleep at the time. But what device had Porky been fitted with? Sorry – TOP SECRET!

The weeks were now ticking by and the big day was approaching fast. Porky had worked hard since the operation, the medical one, and had become fluent in German, received a Royal Pig Air Force grade A in lip reading and passed a rigorous survival course.

There was just time to write a letter to his sweetheart Alice. Of course he couldn't go into any detail of what he had been doing but he could use the space to say how much he loved her and couldn't wait to get back.

'I love you Alice, my darling sweetheart, more than you will ever know, your loving pig Porky xxxxxxxxx.'

Porky placed the letter in its envelope, licked the flap and sealed it tightly. Before he handed it over to a duty officer for posting, he covered the back of the envelope with dozens of kisses.

Tomorrow, Porky would be on his way to a designated area in one remote corner of RAF Spampton. There he would spend two days familiarising himself with the special prepared Lancaster bomber that would drop him behind enemy lines. He would also attend some very important briefings.

Unbeknown to him also was the fact that there would be a lot more surprises in store before he set off across the North Sea to reach his destination. Had Porky known everything, perhaps he would have had second thoughts about putting his name on that piece of paper at Quagmire Hall. On the other hand he may well have done so in any case, after all any young pig of his age would have given his right trotter to be part of this huge adventure.

Doctor Scratchings hurried along the corridor hoping he would reach his office before the phone rang off. Luckily he made it.

'Hello, Doctor Scratchings,' he gasped, almost out of breath. 'Oh Norrie, it's you.'

Norrie Boarwood was yet another inventor who had been working on other things which could result in assisting the war effort greatly.

The doctor listened with interest, 'You mean you have perfected it, that is splendid news, and when will the first batch be ready?'

Like everyone, humans and pigs alike, the work rate was tremendous. What was normally done in a month was now being completed in a week. Working at least sixteen hours per day was the norm in times of war.

Doctor Scratchings could not contain his delight, 'A batch of twenty is ready? Well done Norrie, well done. I will inform Sir Norman immediately.'

Norrie Boarwood, like all inventors, had spent their life trying to come up with something that would leave its mark on society. Now it appeared he may have come up with an invention which could prove very useful and perhaps crucial to the war effort.

The latest inventor had an interest in things electrical and mechanical and started at a very early age. Lying in his straw he was fascinated by the lamp which hung over his head as he snuggled up to his brothers and sisters. Things took a turn also when the farmer brought an old radio into the pig breeding building to listen to during the long days and nights. It was then that Norrie just knew his future lay in – Communications!

Using yet another top secret code E.C.B.S.R.A.T.E. the Exploding Cricket Ball Surveillance Receiver And Transmitter Equipment entered the Second World War just one day before Porky was due to embark on an adventure of a lifetime.

Before Porky set off, there would be a number of hurried changes to the plan set out for him. With the introduction of this new and important device, it was essential that the young pig knew exactly how to use it to its full advantage.

There was also a problem that had reared its head late on in the proceedings. The additional equipment, twenty of the E.C.B.S.R.A.T.E.s meant vacating the Lancaster bomber would prove almost impossible, the hatch was nowhere near wide enough.

Like all problems, especially in times of war, there is always someone who will come up with the solution. Here was no exception, in a very short time a "special arrangement" had been made to ensure Porky would be able to leave the aircraft at the precise moment.

The only problem was that no one had bothered to tell Porky what that special arrangement was. On the other hand, all of this may have been totally intentional!

CHAPTER **8**

Expect a Large Package

The French Resistance Fighters went about their daily routines of causing as much mayhem to their enemy as they could. The Special Truffle Unit carried out daring raids to cause obstruction to supply lines, as was described earlier. Those like Petite Tranches and Maurice Morceau did all in their power to infiltrate the enemy and gather any information they could.

The absence of British activity though was proving costly. Vital information, such as details of the enemy's intended plans, was now non-existent. It was therefore met with great excitement when Petite received information of an "imminent package".

'This has just arrived from the accordionist,' Maurice Morceau informed his friend Petite, handing over a brown envelope.

On this particular day they had chosen a church as their rendezvous point. It was early in the morning and on a Sunday. There was no reason for anyone to suspect anything as it was the normal thing to do in France. The fact that they were the only two in this particular church helped.

Petite Tranches opened the envelope, unfolded the paper inside and read the contents. The sentence at the end of the letter showed just how important the "package" was. The sentence read, "This will be the final attempt!"

Although the letter ended on a downbeat note, the two occupants of the church were nevertheless very excited. Because there had been such a long gap since the last drop of Special Hog Service personnel, both of them knew a lot of planning must have gone into the one that was about to happen. It must be something very special, they both agreed.

'We shall be ready Maurice,' Petite whispered, placing her trotter on his.

Maurice nodded, and affirmed, 'Of course we will.'

Back in the United Kingdom, news of the war wasn't very encouraging. The Germans were advancing across Europe in all directions and every day listeners who had radios, or visitors to cinemas, learned of much loss of life both at home and in the war zones. An awful lot would now fall on the shoulders of one pig!

Of course, life had to go on and the wheels of industry kept turning, especially at Porky's old work place the Spud & Company's Potato Mash Manufacturing factory. On this particular day, though, there was one pretty young pig beaming from ear to ear. She was also brandishing a letter.

'Porky's written,' she mouthed to her work mates. She just couldn't help smiling and kissing the letter.

'He loves me, he still loves me!'

Alice hadn't heard from her sweetheart for ages and she had no idea where and how he was. Thankfully the letter went some way to reassuring her that he was alright. Like Porky, though, she had no idea what was lying ahead for him. She hoped he had received the letter she sent to him the week before.

RAF Spampton looked like any other airfield dotted around the east of England. Large aircraft were coming and going, uniformed pigs dashing here and there in vehicles, on bicycles or by foot. On the runway perimeter, huge bombs were being transported on tractor drawn trolleys towards stationary Lancaster Bombers.

Unlike other airfields, though, a solitary Lancaster stood motionless inside a barbed wire compound with its markings glistening in the early morning sunshine. The aircraft's name proudly standing out, "The City of Brawnton".

Inside a building, not far from the aeroplane, Porky sat motionless with his head bowed and obviously deep in thought. In fact he may not have been aware himself, but he was actually in a state of shock. Wouldn't anybody be that way though having just been told that, because of extra things to carry, he couldn't fit inside the aircraft for the flight?

Due to late developments and the fact that the exploding cricket ball devices would now be part of Porky's equipment, the hatches used to exit the aircraft by parachute wouldn't be wide enough.

'I am terribly sorry about this,' an officer explained. 'But we have made things as comfortable as possible.'

How could hanging from one of the bomb bays for hours on end be made remotely comfortable? Porky would soon find out because that is exactly where he would be throughout the whole of the flight. Not quite outside and open to the elements but as near as makes no difference. It would also be freezing cold!

Porky gave a huge sigh, saying to himself that if you put your name on a piece of paper like he had done, you had to accept the circumstances. Sitting by himself, he had time to reflect, and things didn't look too bright. It should be remembered at this stage Porky also had no idea about the mix up with the Voice Changing Anti Grunting Device.

What if he succeeded with the drop only to be discovered and apprehended thanks to what can only be described as a mix up on somebody's part?

The sound of a vehicle approaching brought Porky to his trotters. Through a small window he could see a large camouflaged car slowing down and grinding to a halt at the opening of the barbed wire compound. As the occupant climbed out Porky recognised him immediately, it was Sir Norman Thyne-Rashers.

Suddenly the young pig felt lifted. If such a high ranking officer had made the effort to visit an ordinary pig, then the whole thing must be worth it.

'Good luck Michael,' Sir Norman said, taking the youngster by the trotter and shaking it firmly.

Porky acknowledged, 'Thank you sir, I will do my best.'

'There is one final thing,' the Air Commodore added, opening a small container. 'I want you to wear this with pride.'

Sir Norman then stepped forward and pinned an insignia on to Porky. "Member of the Special Hog Service" it read!

The Air Commodore then stepped back, saluted smartly then turned and made his way back to the car.

Porky, with a tear in his eye, swallowed hard. A slight discomfort in his throat immediately reminded him of the operation. 'We'll soon know what it's all about,' he said quietly to himself.

There was now just one more thing that required doing and one which can only be described as somewhat bizarre.

'Mr Porkinson, I am Harry Tamworth your painter.'

Porky looked very puzzled at what had just been said, 'Painter?'

'Yes didn't anyone tell you?'

Before Porky could answer, Harry Tamworth continued, 'It's my job to camouflage you. We leave it until the last minute so it is fresh when you land at your destination, now if you will follow me and take your clothes off!'

Bizarre it certainly was, here was a total stranger asking a pig to take his clothes off so he can paint him.

'I've got the documentation if you want confirmation,' the painter called back as he led Porky into what was obviously the paint shop. It was a relatively bare room with the exception of a table full of paint and brushes. There was also a full length mirror in one corner.

'No need for that documentation,' Porky cried. 'All I hope is that the paint is the quick drying sort.'

'It is almost instant,' was the reply.

'Then let's go,' Porky urged. 'And put some colour in my cheeks!'

Both Porky and the painter laughed at this remark. It was just the comment to make at a time like this.

Porky stripped off and Harry Tamworth began.

Within an hour the young pig had been transformed. Walking up to the mirror he examined the painter's work.

'There are a lot of pink pigs in the world,' he said. 'And for that matter black and white ones too, but I can't think there can be many green and khaki ones.'

Porky had dressed again after about half an hour and was leaning against the wall of the building. Suddenly, one by one, the engines of the lonely Lancaster burst into life. It would be the warm up prior to the departure or more precise, the start of the sortie.

This was the signal for Porky to gather his things and be ready for when the final word was given. Priority was given to the two things he had treasured since his pighood, Granddad's helmet and goggles. These two items could prove very useful, especially as now he would be exposed to the outside elements during the flight.

Then there were the exploding cricket balls, plus a supply of receivers and recorders. Porky would have to take a supply of food, enough to last him until he made his rendezvous. Then there was the other piece of essential equipment for any Special Hog Service member, binoculars.

Finally, as well as warm clothing, he needed to carry his survival kit which included pens and paper, and of course, last but not least, his parachute. All in all a large cargo, or should that be a heavy "bomb load".

It was now that the countdown reached its final stage. Porky, fully equipped, was being led to the waiting aircraft. Surrounding him, a large group of ground crew had gathered. Then, from the direction of the control tower, a despatch rider appeared, weaving his motorcycle in and out of stationary vehicles and other aircraft.

Pulling up sharply to where Porky was about to be hoisted into the bomb bay, he jumped from his motorcycle and dashed over to the brave young pig.

'This has just arrived for you,' the despatch rider shouted above the aircraft engines. He then handed over the envelope and returned to his motorcycle.

Porky, looking somewhat puzzled opened the envelope, 'Oh

yes!' he called out at the top of his voice.

Inside the envelope was a photo of the most important pig in his life. It was of Alice, clad in only a negligee. On the back it read. 'Hope this reminds you of the good times to come when you get back. I will love you always, your darling Alice xxxxxxxxx.'

The final piece of military issue was a large blue scarf. He wrapped it round his face to protect him from the cold he would most certainly experience during his flight inside the cold and draughty bomb bay.

At last the time came, attached securely Porky felt the large aircraft move off and start its taxiing around the perimeter. Eventually the Lancaster came to a halt at the end of a long runway. A quick check of the many dials in the cockpit and then the pilot eased the levers, whilst at the same time increasing power to the four engines.

The huge aeroplane began to move forward, steadily at first but then building up speed until he was satisfied it would lift off the ground. At this precise moment the pilot pulled hard on the levers.

From his position in the bomb bay, Porky had just enough vision to see the tarmac below. In a short time the huge chunk of machinery was airborne, next stop for Michael Porkinson, member of the S.H.S, somewhere in France!

CHAPTER 9

Will Porky Give a Hoot?

There was an amount of interest and trepidation amongst the French Resistance fighters who had gathered in the vicinity of the expected drop zone. Petite Tranches, the young female, was included in the selected group simply because she spoke English and had been briefed on the "mysterious cricket balls".

As usual, a number of German soldiers were in the area and being observed very closely. Shortly dusk would descend, signalling the arrival of a very important member of the Special Hog Service. This mission must not fail, which accounted for the high number of resistance fighters who were present at this time. They were heavily armed and had one purpose in common, to stop the enemy from capturing their special visitor.

Because the German army had advanced since the last S.H.S. drop, the terrain would be more open. Except that is for a large wood near to where the drop was to be made. This added to the tenseness, clearly shown on the faces of the waiting group.

A slight error by the bomb aimer, or a sudden gust of wind, could result in Porky being blown off course, and into the wood. That didn't bear thinking about. To land in a tree, in the near dark, could result in broken limbs at best or death at worst.

Suddenly, in the distance, the usual droning sound of a Lancaster bomber filled the air.

'This is it,' one of the fighters whispered, and all eyes looked skyward.

'Now remember, our friend will be very tired after his flight and he must be allowed to rest.'

'Yes Petite,' another colleague called out. 'We know it is our job to protect him while he sleeps.'

The plan was that Porky would be dropped by parachute from the bomb bay. The bomb aimer would release the young pig at a precise time and position. If the calculations were correct, Porky would land near to the wood in soft undergrowth. Providing he was in no danger from German patrols, he would be allowed to sleep until one hour before dawn the next morning.

Then, with precision planning, he would be taken to the Resistance fighter's headquarters, which incidentally was a cleverly prepared underground compound, for debriefing. This of course was a long way off yet.

Back at the aircraft, Porky had to get down from the relative safety of the bomb bay to the given target area. Before that happened, a clever plan was introduced to, hopefully, fool the enemy into thinking the S.H.S. member was on his way down and into their hands.

Whilst it was a long time since the last drop, everyone knew the enemy would link the sound of a Lancaster bomber with that of a previous mission. For that reason, the aircraft would drop decoys, in the shape of sacks of logs, at least two miles past the selected drop zone. Then, as if returning home, the pilot would steer his craft back to the correct intended drop, and at the precise moment give his aimer the word to release Porky.

The bomb aimer confirmed, 'Package gone skipper!'

'Good show, now let's go home.' With that the pilot banked and radioed back to his crew. 'RAF Spampton, here we come.'

As the war progressed many improvements were carried out and one such was the colour of parachutes. Instead of the normal white silk, someone came up with the idea of dying the material to blend with the surroundings.

Dark green seemed appropriate in this case, and Porky was one of the first to be brought down to earth using an inconspicuous parachute. All was fine but what will happen if the young pig is not located by the resistance fighters. Let us remember that Porky had had an operation to stop him grunting.

It was around two thirty in the early morning when Petite and her colleagues were aroused by the sound of Germans

approaching. With Porky now on the ground, it was a tense time. Fortunately there were only two and this was confirmed as they passed the spot where the resistance fighters were lying low.

Suddenly, everyone was disturbed by a noise coming from the wood.

The Germans stopped, 'Did you hear that Hans I think it was an English pig over there?'

'Are you sure?' the second German asked.

'I am pretty sure,' came the response. 'Let's go and investigate.'

There was now a lot of tenseness amongst the Resistance fighters they could have a serious fight on their hands. If it was Porky, and he was discovered, they would need to take action to stop him from being captured. To shoot the enemy would not only be dangerous because of the fear of hitting Porky, but it could attract other Germans in the vicinity. Having trained in unarmed combat they knew what to do.

'There it was again Hans, listen!'

Both Germans stood and listened. Then Fritz, the first German burst out laughing. Suddenly all became clear, the noise they heard was in fact the "Too-whit, too-whoo" of an owl.

'Just wait until we get back to camp,' the second German said, joining in the laughter.

'What do you mean Hans?'

Hans laughed even louder before saying, 'Wait until I tell them you couldn't tell the difference between a pig and an owl.'

'You wouldn't tell them Hans, would you?' Fritz pleaded.

'Wouldn't I?' Hans chuckled. 'Wouldn't I?'

Petite and her colleagues listened as the two Germans continued with their laughter before moving off in the distance.

'Gosh that was close,' Petite muttered to herself and then turning to the others whispered, 'we'll give it a couple of hours or so and then we must try and locate Porky, providing he made it of course.'

Everyone then settled down to relax in the quiet of the night. Quiet that is except for the occasional hooting of the owl which was heard earlier.

Just before dawn, the search for the young pig began. It could prove difficult, though, because of the deep undergrowth. Everybody however remained optimistic. So much was depending on the success of this mission, especially as Porky would be carrying a new "product", which could help them enormously.

The exact planned location of the drop was ironically very close to where the owl was heard. It made sense, therefore, to start the search from there.

Petite and her friends moved slowly through the undergrowth spreading out as they did so. All of a sudden they all leapt back, startled by a loud hoot which echoed across the area. But that wasn't all, everyone gaped open mouthed as before them the saw a huge mound start to move. Then, from out of the mound a brown helmet appeared, followed by a pair of goggles and a blue scarf!

'Porky,' Petite called out. 'Is that you?'

'Oh, er, yes!' Porky replied. 'Gosh I have never been so tired.'

'But the hooting, was that you?'

Porky said, somewhat puzzled, 'Hooting, what are you talking about?'

'Oh never mind,' Petite replied. 'Let's get out of here and into the safety of the headquarters.'

By the middle of the morning Porky had been safely escorted to an underground warren and given a good meal of potato parings and a bowl of fermented wine. Shortly he would be ready to start the mission, but not before instructing and demonstrating the new and exciting product everyone was waiting to see.

'Balls?' One of the fighters asked with a puzzled look on his face.

Porky had produced a considerable number of red balls from a bag and was handing them out together with a small metal box no bigger than a matchbox.

'Cricket balls, to be precise,' the young pig explained. 'But not ordinary ones as you will learn.'

All the resistance fighters, and in particular Petite, were intrigued by what had been said.

'Now if you would be so kind as to walk over there.' Porky asked one of the fighters, and I will walk back this way, and can you sing or recite something?'

There was a strange look coming from everyone, but, as there was obviously a purpose to it, the selected fighter started to sing. Porky then took one of the balls and tossed it towards him. 'Keep singing,' Porky said. 'Keep singing.'

As soon as the ball hit the ground it shattered into a cloud of dust. 'Don't stop,' Porky continued. 'Keep singing!'

At the same time as throwing the ball, young Porky had taken the small metal box and was holding it towards the singing.

After a short time Porky called out, 'OK, you can come back now.'

As soon as the fighter who had been singing returned, and with everyone moving up closer, Porky pressed a lever at the side of the small box. They all gasped, then nodded in appreciation

87

and finally smiled as the sound of the fighter's singing came out of the box.

Porky beamed proudly. 'My friends, I give you the Exploding Cricket Ball Surveillance Receiver and Transmitter Equipment or more commonly known as the E.C.B.S.R.A.T.E.'

The young pig continued, 'This is the new weapon that will help us all to monitor troop and ammunition movement, and to gather other vital information. It will help the Truffle Unit to carry out disruption raids and halt enemy progress.'

No sooner had Porky finished when every resistance fighter stood up and applauded.

As for Porky, with the demonstration done, it was time for his last piece of rest before venturing deep into enemy territory. His lip reading skills, his grasp of the German language and his cricket skills would prove so important in acquiring vital information that otherwise may not have been forthcoming.

Why mention cricket skills? Well a "cricket ball" in the right trotter could be tossed a long distance, and if need be high in the air to clear security fencing put up by the enemy.

The brilliant idea of the exploding ball meant that no one would suspect the hearing device. The tiny transmitter in the ball was no bigger than a piece of grit found on any road. Blending in, it was doubtful if anyone would ever spot it. Hats off to Norrie Boarwood, the inventor.

With another consignment of the balls already on their way, things were beginning to look a lot brighter.

Porky retired to a small room just off the main corridor and settled down, knowing that from now on rest and sleep could be in short supply.

Whilst the young pig caught up on his lost sleep, the Resistance Fighters prepared for their next venture. With the new equipment all were now confident of success and the thought of being able to listen to the enemy was very exciting.

Whoever thought a cricket ball would become such a vital piece of equipment?

Now they were all ready to move out, except Petite that is, who would stay behind and assist Porky when he finally awoke.

'Good luck my friends,' Petite called out as her colleagues moved to the exit.

'Thank you Petite,' the leader acknowledged. 'We hope to see you soon.'

Actually it didn't quite turn out as expected because all at once there was a familiar sound coming from inside the compound. 'Tu-whit, tu –whoo!'

And it was coming from the compound where Porky was resting.

'Porky?' Petite gasped. 'It's Porky!'

The others turned and made their way into the small room where the young pig had retired to.

'Quickly,' one of the fighters called out. 'Throw one of those cricket balls.'

'What on earth for?' another asked.

The first one replied, 'Because if we don't record it no one will believe it.'

With that he exploded the ball and then handed the small box to Petite.

'Play it back to Porky when he wakes up, he may not believe you otherwise.'

Petite took the box and then watched as her colleagues left, chuckling to themselves.

CHAPTER 10

Famous in Barnsley
(and the World)

It was 1945 and every street in every town and village was decorated with bunting and flags. Food was also plentiful in supply, despite information broadcast to the contrary. It really was a happy time, it was the end of the war!

For one particular street there would be a special celebration party. It would be in honour of a very special and brave pig. The pig of course was their own Porky. What he had done and what had been achieved was being acknowledged by everyone, including the Prime Minister no less.

There were also more reasons for celebration, but first Porky had an appointment at Quagmire Hall. The purpose for the visit was to seek an explanation why he finished up sounding like an owl, albeit only when he slept.

Lord Hogsby welcomed the heroic pig and ironically entertained him in his study, the place where Porky put his

name on a piece of paper a long time ago. Also present was Doctor Scratchings, who carried out the operation to his throat.

The Doctor really had no explanation how the error had happened. Maybe it was a donor card mix up, perhaps the number six on a container was misread as a number nine. There just wasn't a lot to go on except just after the operation a mute owl was reported as being seen, but not heard, in a barn not far from Sheffield.

If it can be confirmed as the same owl admitted to the animal and bird compound in Quagmire Hall at the same time as Porky's operation those many months ago, then the mystery may be solved.

'We can always try and revert your Hoot to a Grunt,' Doctor Scratchings offered.

'Can you guarantee complete success?'

The doctor shook his head, 'Not one hundred per cent.' Came the response.

'Then we'll leave things as they are,' Porky stated, somewhat disappointed but taking heart that at least he could talk. Not like the poor old owl up there near Sheffield.

And so it was, not only had Porky returned home a hero but he would become a celebrity for two reasons. Firstly as a brave, brave hero and secondly as the only pig in the world who could mimic an owl, albeit only when he was asleep.

There was now, one final mission for Porky to accomplish. It concerned a small church just outside Barnsley.

'Do you Alice Swizzell take Michael "Porky" Porkinson to be your lawful wedded partner?'

Alice looked first at Porky and then turned to face the vicar. 'I do,' she sighed.

'And do you Porky take Alice Swizzell to be your lawful wedded partner?'

Porky smiled and then nodded, 'I do.'

This time it was the turn of the vicar to smile as he squeaked, 'Then I pronounce you Pig and Wife.'

With the ceremony complete the newlyweds hot trottered it to that special street where a long day and night of celebrations were about to begin.

'Ladies and Gentlepigs, I ask you to raise your bowls and drink a toast to Porky and Alice.'

Porky was so happy, he pushed his snout against his new wife's and they embraced passionately.

The young brave pig closed his eyes and said under his breath, 'Mission Accomplished!'

Postscript

Having read detailed accounts of such a very brave animal, there was no wonder that Sir Winston Churchill announced. 'I like Pigs!'

He obviously knew more about them than the rest of us. Perhaps there is more to learn, because as we know a lot of things concerning the Government and the Ministry of Defence remain classified information and stay secret for years and years.

There could be some more very interesting reading when restrictions are eventually lifted.

All that is asked is, until then, if you hear the hoot of an owl, shout a big 'Hello,' because you never know it might be t'lad from Barnsley!

THE END